Miles McHale, TATTLETALE

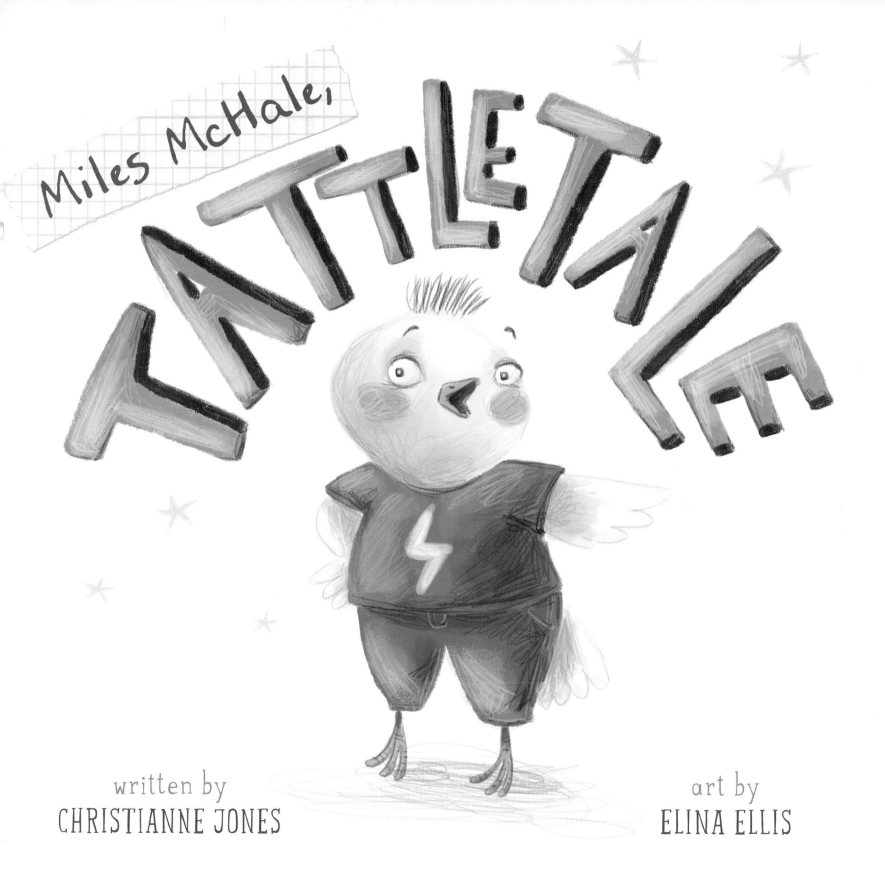

written by
CHRISTIANNE JONES

art by
ELINA ELLIS

PICTURE WINDOW BOOKS
a capstone imprint

Miles McHale, Tattletale is published by
Picture Window Books, a Capstone imprint
1710 Roe Crest Drive, North Mankato, Minnesota 56003
www.mycapstone.com

Library of Congress Cataloging-in-Publication Data
is available on the Library of Congress website.

ISBN 978-1-5158-0753-7 (paper over board)
ISBN 978-1-5158-0752-0 (library binding)
Designed by Aruna Rangarajan

Printed in China.
009991S17

To Emma, Allie, Thomas, Nolan, Kale, Elsa,
Adalyn, and Landon. Don't be tattletales. — CJ

To my darling boy, Sasha Ellis. — Elina Ellis

Miles McHale was smart.
He was funny. He was sweet.

But Miles McHale was also a **TATTLETALE** –
and not just a one-or-two-times-a-day tattler.

We're talking about
CONSTANT
tattling, all day long.

Sometimes, the tattling didn't even stop at bedtime.

The tattling was a
problem at home.

But it was a BIG problem at school.

And Miles wasn't the only tattler.
(But he was the **worst** one.)
So one day, Mrs. Snitcher started the

TATTLE BATTLE.

"Okay, class," Mrs. Snitcher said.

"The rules are simple:
two teams, one week, no tattling.

Whichever team has the
fewest number of tattles gets
EXTRA RECESS on Friday."

When the teams were assigned,
Miles didn't stop tattling.

"Adalyn is being too loud!"

"Lola won't stop clapping!"

"Landon is standing on one foot!"

His team was NOT impressed.

"Miles, hold on a minute," Mrs. Snitcher said. "Before we start, let's recite the **TATTLE BATTLE PLEDGE.**"

If a friend is sick, hurt, or in harm's way, then telling someone is OKAY.

And with that, the Tattle Battle
officially began.

Miles knew the rules, and he didn't want to let his team down. But sometimes it was hard to know what was tattling and what wasn't.

"Is she sick or hurt or in danger?" Mrs. Snitcher asked.

"Well . . . she could choke on it," Miles replied.

"True. But that's not likely."

"Okay," Miles said. "Got it."

"Is she sick or hurt or in danger?"
Mrs. Snitcher asked.

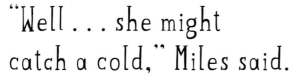

"Well . . . she might
catch a cold," Miles said.

"Maybe. But that's not likely."

"Okay," Miles said. "Got it."

But he didn't really get it.

He tried hard, but Miles kept letting his team down. By the
end of the week, his team was losing, and he was alone.

Alone at recess.

Alone at lunch.

And alone on his walk home.

Nobody wanted to talk to him — especially his teammates. His team was losing the Tattle Battle, and it was all his fault.

"That's it," he said to himself.

"No more tattling. EVER."

That night, Miles was playing in his room
when he heard a loud noise in the kitchen.

"Hattie, what happened?" Miles asked.

"I wanted another cookie," his sister said. "But when I climbed onto the counter, I slipped."

Miles had a choice to make. Should he tell his mom or not? He didn't want to be a tattletale, but Hattie was hurt.

Then Miles remembered the **TATTLE BATTLE** pledge:

If a friend is sick, hurt, or in harm's way, then telling someone is OKAY.

The next day, the class recited the Tattle
Battle pledge right after the first bell.

If a friend is sick, hurt, or in harm's way, then telling someone is okay.

But at the end of the pledge, Miles McHale went on:

Unless it's sickness, danger, or bullying I see, I will mind my own business and worry about me.

"Miles McHale! That is a wonderful addition to our pledge!" Mrs. Snitcher said. "I will take away three tattle points for your team."

Miles **beamed** with pride. His team still lost the Tattle Battle, but that was okay. He apologized to his team and won back his friends.

After that day Miles McHale never tattled
again. In fact, nobody ever tattled again.
Life was perfect.

THE END.